Gekko Saves the City

Based on the episode
"Lionel-saurus"

Ready-to-Read

Simon Spotlight
New York   London   Toronto   Sydney   New Delhi

SIMON SPOTLIGHT
An imprint of Simon & Schuster Children's Publishing Division
1230 Avenue of the Americas, New York, New York 10020
This Simon Spotlight edition October 2020
Adapted by May Nakamura from the series PJ Masks
All rights reserved, including the right of reproduction in whole or in part in any form.
SIMON SPOTLIGHT, READY-TO-READ, and colophon are registered trademarks of Simon & Schuster, Inc.
For information about special discounts for bulk purchases, please contact Simon & Schuster Special Sales at 1-866-506-1949 or business@simonandschuster.com.
Manufactured in the United States of America 1020 LAK
10 9 8 7 6 5 4 3 2 1
ISBN 978-1-5344-1774-8 (eBook)
ISBN 978-1-5344-7332-4 (prop)

Greg loves playing with
his pet lizard, Lionel.

Oh no!

Lionel is gone!

The PJ Masks need to find him!

Amaya becomes Owlette!

Greg becomes Gekko!

Connor becomes Catboy!

They are the PJ Masks!

The PJ Masks hear
a loud noise.

They run toward the sound.

Now the sound is coming
from behind them.

Who is there?

It is Lionel!

He is as big as a house!

Romeo gives strange treats
to Lionel.

Lionel grows even bigger!

"Lionel is out of control,"
says Catboy.
"He needs a leash,"
says Owlette.

Gekko thinks a leash is
a bad idea.

Lionel does not like

the leash.

He shakes it off.

Romeo wants Lionel to destroy Headquarters. "Climb!" Romeo says to Lionel.

Oh no!

Headquarters will fall down!

Gekko feels bad.

He should not have

put a leash on Lionel.

Lionel and Gekko are friends.

Gekko has an idea.

He grabs a tree branch

with his Super Lizard Grip.

"Fetch, Lionel!"

Gekko says.

Lionel loves playing fetch!

He leaps off Headquarters.

"No!" Romeo wails.

His plan is ruined.

Lionel shrinks back
to his normal size.

"I love you, Lionel!"

Gekko says.

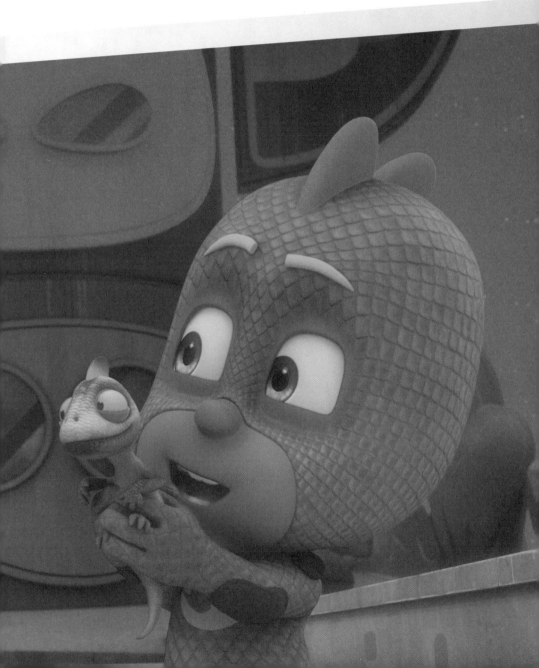

The PJ Masks save the day
and Lionel, too!